SHONTO BEGAY

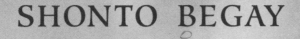

'Ma'ii and Cousin Horned Toad

A TRADITIONAL NAVAJO STORY

SCHOLASTIC
HARDCOVER

SCHOLASTIC INC. ♦ New York

Up on the mountainside, where the air smells like cedar and pine, Ma'ii paused, and looked back into the sagebrush-covered valley.

He was glad to be away from there. Sagebrush made his nose itch.

He had been trotting along all morning. The sun was now directly over his head. He was hungry. Ma'ii was always hungry.

I think I'll visit my cousin on the other side of the mountain, he thought. *I know he'll feed me good.*

As he ran, his stomach growled. He liked his stomach full, not noisy.

Meanwhile, cousin Horned Toad was out pulling weeds in his cornfield. Wiping sweat off his forehead, he sang while he worked:

"*Working every day in my cornfield*
Tending it with care
Praying every day in my cornfield
That rain will fill the air
Soon I'll harvest my cornfield
My bounty I'll share
When snow covers my cornfield
Warmth and joy with many fine meals
Friends, neighbors and — "

"Hey, cousin!" Horned Toad's song was interrupted as Ma'ii came crashing through the cornfield. "I haven't seen you in a long while!" he exclaimed as he shook Horned Toad's entire body in a rough, coyote-style handshake. Then Ma'ii noticed the tall corn stalks. He could almost taste those plump, juicy, young ears of corn.

"Welcome to my —" Horned Toad started to say, but Ma'ii rudely interrupted him again, begging Horned Toad to share his corn with his poor, hungry, long-lost cousin.

Horned Toad knew he had work to do. But being the nice fellow he was, he scampered off into the cornfield. And back he came, with a sackful of corn.

After a meal of delicious roast corn and squash stew, Ma'ii sat back and rubbed his big, full stomach. He licked his lips and paws. "My, that was a good appetizer," he said. "And if you wouldn't mind, my dear cousin, I am ready for the main course."

Horned Toad was mad. He'd worked hard to grow all this food. But being the nice fellow he was, he just scampered back into the cornfield once again and returned a short while later with another sackful of corn.

As soon as the ears of corn were roasted, Ma'ii gobbled them down without so much as a thank-you.

Horned Toad grew madder by the moment. Before Ma'ii could ask him for any more food, Horned Toad wagged his finger and scolded, "Cousin, you certainly eat way too much. If you must eat again, you will work in my cornfield."

Ma'ii hated working more than anything. That was why he traveled from one cousin to the next — for food and a place to sleep. With great reluctance, Ma'ii began to pull weeds and water the cornfield. But then he decided to drink the rest of the water himself.

After Horned Toad was out of sight, Ma'ii lay down in the shade of a big cornstalk. He thought how wonderful it would be to own a farm like this. Why, he wouldn't have to travel. He would just sit there in the brush hut and roast corn all day long. As he thought, he sang a soft song.

"Hey nay ya ho ye'
Hey nay ya ho ye'
I've been blessed with a cornfield this day
I've stopped my running and begging this day
Mother Earth has provided me with
Endless food this day
For I am the child of Ye'ii
Hey nay ya ho ye'
Hey nay ya ho ye'
Sweet smell of roast corn will fill the air
And carry my prayer to Father Sun above
To bless me some more
For I am the child of Ye'ii
Hey nay ya ho ye'"

As he sang, he schemed of a way to trick his cousin out of his farm. Ma'ii had lots of tricks that he had learned on his journeys. So he decided to fake a pain in his mouth.

"Help, cousin!" screamed Ma'ii. *"Waa oooh! Wee ooh ooh!"*

Horned Toad dropped what he was doing and came running.
"What has happened, cousin?" he asked.

"I have a piece of hard corn stuck between my teeth," Ma'ii
moaned. "Way back there, and I can't get to it . . . if only you could
just climb into my mouth, perhaps you could wiggle it free and save
me from this terrible pain! *Owww waa oooh!*"

Well, Horned Toad didn't really want to climb into Ma'ii's mouth.
But being the nice fellow he was, he climbed all the way inside anyway.

SNAP!
Ma'ii's mouth closed tight and, just as fast,
he swallowed his small cousin.
Then Ma'ii looked around at Horned Toad's farm.
It was all his.

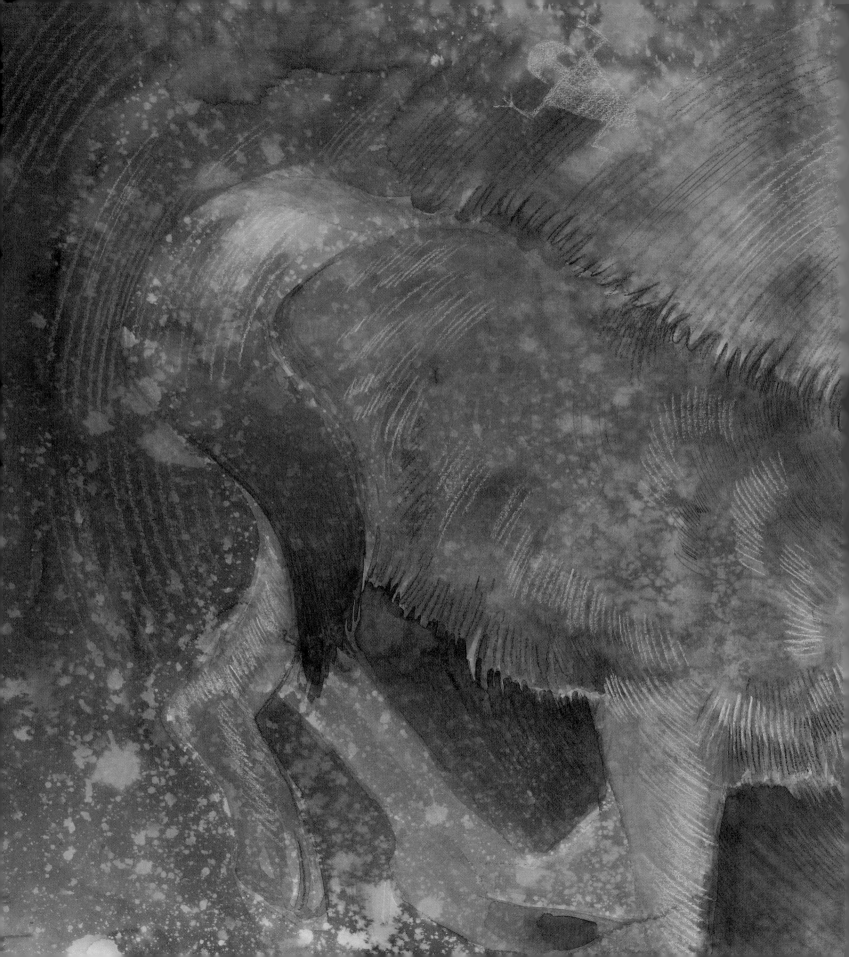

That afternoon, Ma'ii had another big meal of roast corn and squash stew. Then he fell asleep with a big grin on his face. But his sleep was brief.

"*Shil na aash. Shil na aash . . .*"

A strange, faraway voice awakened Ma'ii. He rubbed his eyes and looked about. "Sounds like someone is saying, 'My cousin. My cousin,' " he said to himself. "It is probably just a dream. It happens like that sometimes after a big meal."

Ma'ii rolled over and went back to sleep. But no sooner was he asleep again than the faraway voice returned.

"*Shil na aash* . . ."

This time, Ma'ii jumped up and raced around the brush hut. "Show yourself! Who is it?" he yelled.

Ma'ii was a superstitious fellow. He didn't like to be frightened. But now he was sure that cousin Horned Toad's spirit had come to haunt him. *Yee yah!*

Ma'ii fled to the other side of the cornfield. There he found a safe spot under a big juniper tree, where he fell asleep again. But no sooner was he asleep than the faraway voice returned.

"*Shil na aash.* It is me, Horned Toad. I am in your stomach," came the voice from deep inside of Ma'ii.

"B-But . . . " sputtered Ma'ii. "I-I thought you were —"

"No, cousin," said Horned Toad. "I am fine. It's nice and warm in here. All the food I need and more keeps coming down. And best of all, I don't have to pull weeds. . . . But I would like to pull out these sharp things that are poking me in the side."

"*Ouch!*" yelped Ma'ii. "Those are my ribs!"

"Ahhh," sighed Horned Toad. "I think I found home."
And he stretched himself out in a nice, cozy spot.

"Listen," hissed Ma'ii. "You come out this instant,
or I'll drown you out."

"Oh, please, don't do that," said Horned Toad. "Please
don't drown me."

But Ma'ii ignored his cousin's plea. He ran down to the
creek and drank until he could hold no more. Then he smiled.
He was rid of Horned Toad now.

"Water's good down here," came the small voice inside
of Ma'ii. "And, thank you. The cornmeal was making me quite
thirsty. Cornmeal does that, you know."

Ma'ii was getting mad. "Come out right now or I will burn you out!" he growled.

But Horned Toad just yawned. "And give up this good life in here? Oh, no, not me."

Now Ma'ii was so mad he ran to the fire and stood over it with all four legs spread apart. The flames licked his stomach and scorched his hair and skin.

"*Oow oow ouch!*" Ma'ii yelped.

"Many thanks, cousin," Horned Toad called out. "Now I have a nice, warm bath and hot cornmeal!"

Ma'ii was the maddest yet. "Come out here right now or I will crush you!" screamed Ma'ii as he ran towards the edge of the canyon. Just as he was about to jump, he realized that this may not be a good idea.

"Listen, cousin," Ma'ii pleaded. "Come out now and we will settle this together."

"But I'm so comfortable in here," Horned Toad insisted. "I don't think I shall ever leave."

"Dear cousin, please. If you come out right now, you can have your farm back. I will leave at once and never bother you again."

"I would rather go exploring. After all, this is my new home," said Horned Toad.

Horned Toad's skin was too rough for Ma'ii's delicate insides. He swam through the tunnels and strange spaces inside of Ma'ii until he came upon Ma'ii's big, fat, thumping heart. Ma'ii screamed and begged for mercy.

Horned Toad gave Ma'ii's heart one big tug, then another. Ma'ii yelped and fell to the ground. He had fainted from fright.

Later that evening, Horned Toad crawled out through Ma'ii's mouth. Ma'ii was still out cold. Horned Toad took Ma'ii's big, greasy tongue and gave it a gigantic pull.

Ma'ii's eyes opened and he bolted to his feet. He let out a frightful scream and ran off into the dusk without ever looking back once.

And even to this day, Ma'ii leaves
his cousin Horned Toad alone.

About the Coyote and the Horned Toad

Among the Navajo, Coyote has many names. In our stories of Coyote as trickster and mischief maker, we call him Ma'ii. He also has many faces. In some of our stories he is a hero. Sometimes he is a villain. In some stories he is brave and in others he is cowardly. *Ma'ii Jol Dlooshi'* or "Coyote out walking stories" are teaching tales. These stories show us proper ways to conduct ourselves. They also explain natural phenomena, but they are always pure entertainment.

Whenever we come upon a horned toad, we gently place it over our heart and greet it. *"Ya ateeh shi che"* ("Hello, my grandfather"). We believe it gives strength of heart and mind. We never harm our grandfather.

Glossary of Navajo Words*

WORD	PRONUNCIATION	TRANSLATION
Ahéhee'	(A*HYEH*hay)	Thank you
Hágoónee'	(Ha*go*NAY)	Good-bye
Mạ'ii	(Ma*EEH)	Coyote
Shil na aash	(Sheelsh na ash)	My cousin
Shi che	(Shee chay)	My grandfather
Yá'át'ééh	(YAH*ah*t*eh)	A greeting, like hello
Yee yah!	(Yee yah)	An expression of fright
Ye'ii	(Yeh*EEH)	Navajo deity (one of the most important ones)

* When Navajo is written, the words contain tone marks as they appear in the "word" column of the glossary. We have, however, left the tone marks out of the text in the story to make reading easier for children.

Library of Congress Cataloging-in-Publication Data

Begay, Shonto.
Ma'ii and cousin Horned Toad: a traditional Navajo story /
retold and illustrated by Shonto Begay.
p.   cm.
Summary: A lazy, conniving coyote takes advantage
of his cousin Horned Toad, until Horned Toad teaches him a lesson he never forgets.
ISBN 0-590-45391-2
1. Navajo Indians—Legends. 2. Coyote (Legendary character)
3. Horned toads—Folklore. [1. Navajo Indians—Legends.
2. Indians of North American—Legends. 3. Coyotes—Folklore.
4. Horned toads—Folklore.] I. Title.
E99.N3B434   1992
398.2'089972—dc20   91-34888
[E]   CIP
AC

12 11 10 9 8 7 6 5 4 3 2   3 4 5 6 7/9
Printed in the U.S.A.   36
First Scholastic Printing, November 1992
Design by Claire B. Counihan
The illustrations in this book
were done with watercolor, gouache,
color pencil, and magic on
color illustration
board.

Dedicated
to the spirit of *Dineh*
To the elders, our strength and courage
To the youth, our hope and promises
and to all those that share
in our dreams and struggles
To my grandmother,
Bessie Smith,
1875–1988